Publisher's Cataloging in Publication Data

Meridian. Volume four : Coming Home / Writer: Barbara Kesel; Penciler: Steve McNiven ; Inker: Tom
Simmons ; Colorist: Morry Hollowell.

p. : ill. ; cm.

Spine title: Meridian. 4 : Coming Home

ISBN: 1-931484-38-4

1. Fantasy fiction. 2. Adventure fiction. 3. Graphic novels. 4. Sephie (Fictitious character) I. Kesel,
Barbara. II. McNiven, Steve. III. Simmons, Tom. IV. Hollowell, Morry. V. Title: Coming Home VI. Title:
Meridian. 4 :Coming Home.

PN6728 .S47 2002
813.54 [Fic]

MERIDIAN ®

Coming Home

Barbara **KESEL**
WRITER

Steve **McNIVEN**
PENCILER

Tom **SIMMONS**
INKER

Morry **HOLLOWELL**
COLORIST

CHAPTER 22

Andy **SMITH** - PENCILER
Mark **FARMER** - INKER
Jeremy **COX** - COLORIST

Troy **PETERI** - LETTERER

CrossGeneration Comics   **Oldsmar, Florida**

Coming Home

features Chapters 21 - 26
of the ongoing series
MERIDIAN

MERIDIAN ®

Far away... on the world of Demetria, explosions rocked the surface and gigantic rocks shot into the sky and stayed there. Settlers established great city-states on these ore-buoyant islands, using floating ships to move between them.

One of these islands is Meridian, home of shipbuilders and Sephie, the daughter of Minister Turos. Sephie's life has been spent being groomed to someday take over the ruling of Meridian. Her uncle Ilahn is the Minister of the rich city-state of Cadador, which controls most of the shipping and trade on Demetria.

When a mysterious force endows both brothers with the Sigil, a link to power, Turos (weakened by Ilahn's poisoning) dies, and his sigil is transferred to Sephie.

Ilahn gains the power to speed decay and create destruction. Sephie finds she has the power to force renewal, allowing her to heal, propel herself through the sky, and move things without touching them.

Ilahn tries, and fails, to control Sephie. Now he wants to gain control of all Demetria, beginning with his conquest of the island where he was born: Meridian.

Sephie's quest to rally support against Ilahn takes her to the waters

Story So Far

surrounding Massintak, the step city, accompanied by a trio of loggers, a few caverns dwellers, and Deren Beq, whose stories of Sephie are outracing their flight, bringing them new volunteers. Sephie is reunited with Jad, who has brought a small crew from Hesperia because of a vision from the Muse of Giatan. Romance is blossoming between Sephie and Jad, although Jad's been warned against *distracting* her.

Sephie's pirates, aided by new inventions from Massintak, have been successfully harassing the ships on Cadador's trade route to prove Ilahn can be stopped. A messenger from the ironworking island of Torbel causes them to abandon their blockade and rush to the rescue.

Meanwhile, Ilahn, plotting with Reesha and Rho Rhustane, has sent Rho to Meridian to oversee the construction of a new ship and control the remaining population. Ilahn is enforcing the embargo on the ore that keeps Torbel aloft, dooming the heavy island.

Ilahn's armada is sent to dispatch the pirates, but it is the armada that is decimated by Sephie and Samandahl Rey, another Sigil-Bearer, but one who hails from another world. Sam appears from nowhere and leaves as mysteriously, but not before he and Sephie have touched minds, giving her a wealth of information, both tactical and personal.

I was shaken by the impact -- it'd scattered us all -- but more shaken when I realized there was no other sign of movement.

We were **HERE** on this coast because it was the most convenient place for me to tend to the injured Cadadorians. **THEY** were hurt because I'd been leading raids against Ilahn's forces.

For one terrible long moment, I thought I'd killed them all.

...before it hit the ground.

Pure terror.

My thoughts scattered like startled birds...

...leaving only empty fear.

There had to be a way around the pulsing fear...

...I just had to THINK!

Think like SAM...

"...*THIS* ONE BELONGS TO SEPHIE."

Given the choice, I'd much rather negotiate than strike out with my hands.

That comes from being raised by loving people in a gentle land.

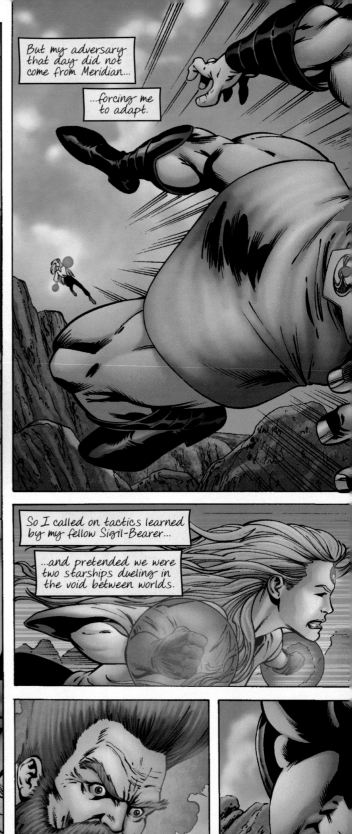

But my adversary that day did not come from Meridian...

...forcing me to adapt.

So I called on tactics learned by my fellow Sigil-Bearer...

...and pretended we were two starships dueling in the void between worlds.

KRAKT

Making it a game allowed me to step outside the madness he spawned in me and dispassionately analyze his actions.

To NOTICE that he avoided being touched by me.

My thumping heart leaped with a wild pride at my boldness.

He attempted to misdirect my attention by igniting another explosion from the cannon...

...but I wasn't a CHILD.

Now that I knew what his weapon did, I knew also that I could counter its force.

I was arrogant and prideful, lost in the lofty heights of my self-satisfaction...

...THE CANNON.

I wish it had never been created, but it was THERE and SOLID and there was NO returning to the moment before its existence.

If Ilahn ever gained control of its power, he'd certainly use it to subjugate new territories.

He'd become Demetria's overlord.

Yet, if WE took control of this weapon's terrible power...

...would that be any better?

The choice was painful and difficult...

...because there was no right decision.

It had been replaced by a travesty of benign leadership in the form of an invasion force from Cadador.

They hadn't governed Meridian in my absence...

...they'd raped it.

But I'd learned to FIGHT.

Meridian was mine by right of birth.

It didn't matter that ILAHN had claimed regency until I came of age. I had faced his trade forces, his special soldiers, and his power-wielding friend Rho...

MERIDIAN WILL STILL BE HERE WHEN YOU WAKE.

"NOT *ONLY* CAN SEPHIE *FLY,* BUT SHE CAN SEND OUT *WAVES,* LIKE THE WIND!

"SHE *PUSHED* OUR SHIPS BACK TO MASSINTAK FROM TORBEL!

"THEN THE *CADADORIAN ARMADA* ATTACKED--

"AND THIS GUY FROM *ANOTHER WORLD*--

"THEN--

"*BOOM!*

"THE *CANNONBALL* STRUCK, DESTROYING MOST OF OUR SHIPS!

"AND SEPHIE BATTLED THE WEAPON'S OWNER, RHO RHUSTANE, SINGLE-HANDEDLY--"

My first night home was spent tossing in troubled un-sleep.

I chased rest, but couldn't find it in an unfamiliar bed in my so very familiar world.

Giving up any illusion of slumber, I crawled out to greet the sunrise...

...just as I used to do.

But I'd never met morning alone before...

Papa had always been there.

Now he shines among the stars.

...survives.

I never did get any sleep until it was all over...

...the day I killed Ilahn.

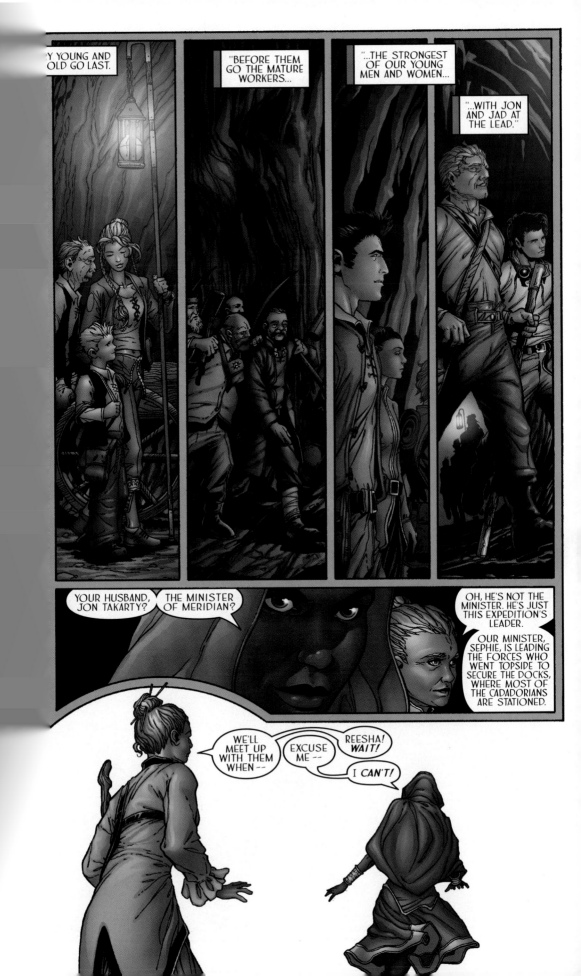

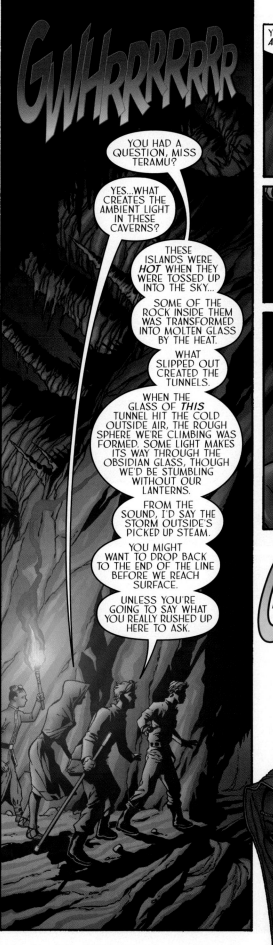

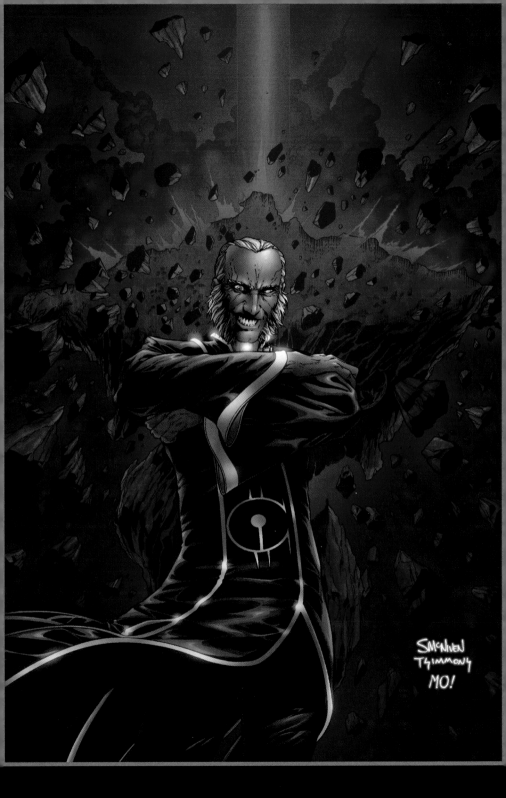

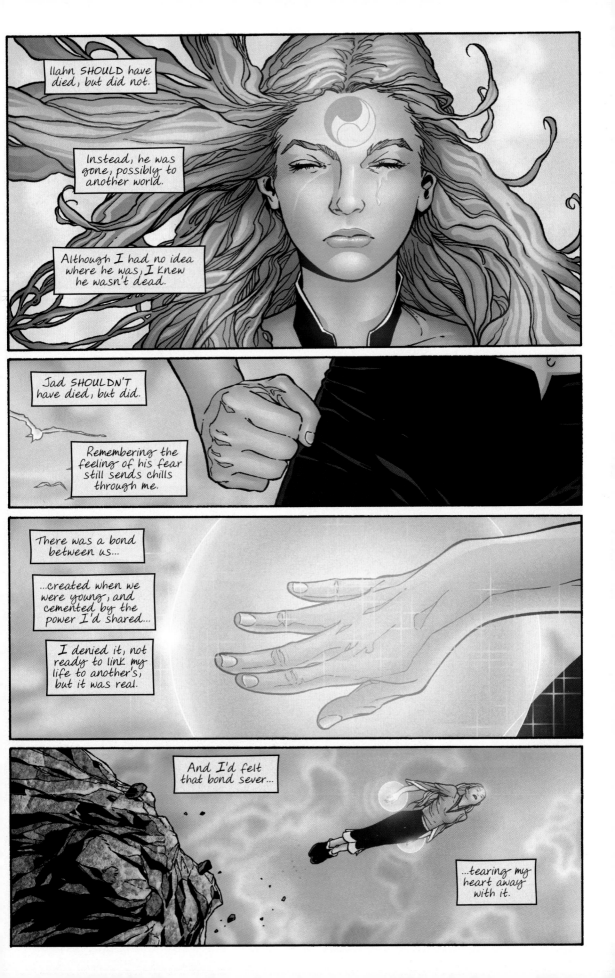

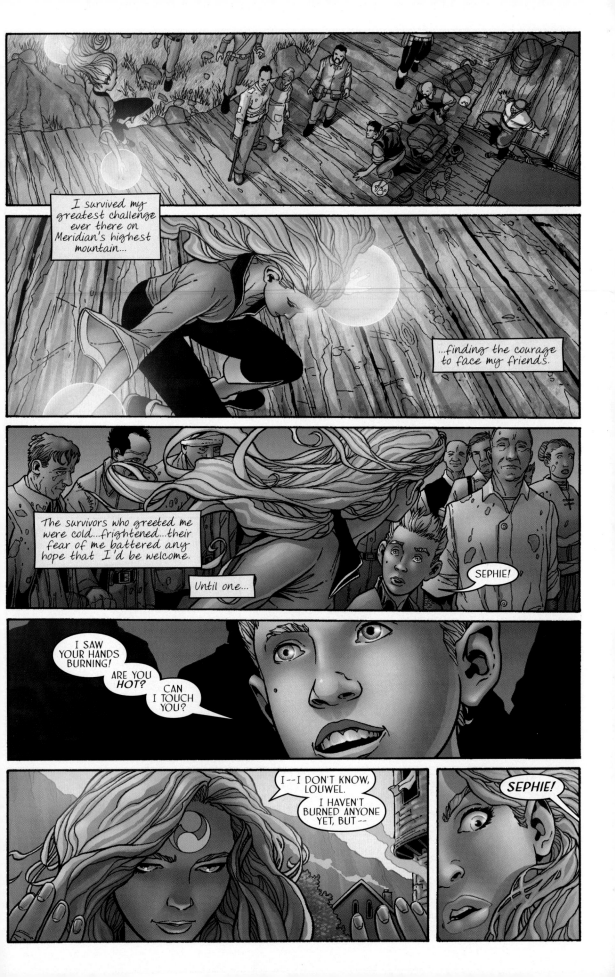

The Tides of Wind

A Journal of events as witnessed or learned by Laolara Mardrin of Ring City

Extraordinary days have come to Ring City. Our little circle of rocks will go down in history as one of the first places to know the news of the mysterious transformation of Sephie of Meridian and Ilahn of Cadador. I am making this book so my children will know what it was like to be present when the world itself was forever changed.

As I write this, I am not yet twenty years of age. My father, Poul, and my mother, Rhietta, are leather toolers. They add the decorative touches to covers and spines. We live on the sixth island of the nine that form the ring.

Our combined island (for Ring City is a chain, not a single sky island) was formed through hard labor. Dissidents who could not abide Cadador's strict laws and intellectuals who prized unfettered thought above all other freedoms joined to begin the work of collecting and chaining islands of a "useless" size. Chaining and tethering these stray rocks created the cooperative island we call home. Differences united us; our unity will sustain us.

Ring City is the home of books. On each of the sister islands, a different function contributing to the creation and sale of books, both text and blank, is housed. The island of pulpers trails the rest, its effluvia contained by the rogue winds from the east. It is only on days of doldrums that Ring City's people regret our trade and think longingly of others — the smell of settling pulp makes pig farming seem a delectable profession.

Our first hint of the biggest event to affect Demetria since the Cataclysm came when a small trade ship stopped here after leaving the island of Meridian. We heard the strange tale of Minister Turos' death, which was followed by the supernatural marking of his brother, Ilahn of Cadador, and daughter Sephie. That very same night, the Ministry of Meridian burned to the ground and the daughter of Meridian disappeared.

A Ministry ship from Torbel stopping on its way from Cadador continued the strange tale. Mysterious lights were spotted coming from the Ministry there and Sephie was seen at the side of Minister Ilahn. The representative from Torbel, an iron-legged man named

Trupert, seemed so sad. Ilahn was playing negotiation games with him the likes of which he hadn't been prepared to challenge, and he feared he'd failed his island. But he feared only economic woes, not the horrifying fate awaiting Torbel.

Torbel, you may remember, is the island that fell from the sky. It was a city of ironworkers, a heavy island buoyed by hundreds of ore pods. When Ilahn cut off their source of ore, it was only a matter of time before the inevitable occurred — the island of Torbel now lies under the sickening waters. Her people are refugees in search of a new home. Many of them have joined Sephie's Pirates of the Wind.

You'll have to forgive me — I'm getting ahead of myself.

So, having learned that Sephie was now living on Cadador, we feared yet expected that the dynamic engine of corruption that is Cadador would consume and corrupt little Meridian. News came of ships, one after another, depositing more Cadadorian soldiers on Meridian's peaceful surface. Reports came of the shipbuilders still on the island (many had fled when the first soldiers arrived) being forced to labor on some unimaginable new craft.

Poor Meridian. Her Minister (still not legally so, Sephie being so young) was trapped in Cadador, unable to prevent the damage done to her island.

We of Ring City found ourselves drawn into the tension when our friends from Meridian came seeking shelter after leaving their home island. Ring City has always been neutral — a stubborn philosophy with self-preservation at its core — so although we took them in, we hid them in the Ministry, making them virtual prisoners without bars or guards, because Cadador's reach extended to Ring City: Cadadorian soldiers came here, too. We feared not bloodshed but loss of crucial trade if the Meridianites were discovered after the Cadadorians had "requested" our assistance in watching for them.

Those were tense times; a simple stroll to market became an exercise in not allowing one's eyes to rest for too long on the supposedly empty Ministry building. We staged readings and plays to divert the Cadadorians' attention from noises and motions where none should be. We tried to carry on as if nothing whatsoever had changed from the day before the Cadadorians came, and we met for secret votes to determine if we should ask the Meridianites to move on. I am proud to say we voted, almost to a man, not to request their departure. During all that time, my hands trembled and my fingernails were bitten to the quick, but I did my part to help. When the Meridianites were indeed discovered, we did hesitate, but quickly sided with the refugees. Your mother, you will be pleased to know, can handle herself in a fight. Soon after, the Meridianites departed to settle a new, wild island.

Then came the most shocking news: we heard of Sephie's death, her fall to the surface after Cadadorian soldiers intercepted her attempt to escape Ilahn. We mourned: Sephie had been a friend to Ring City and we assumed she would continue the good practices initiated by her father. When the rumors came from the surface — that Sephie had somehow survived her fall — we hoped they were true.

Then the stories became wilder. Sephie was spotted at various venues along the western coast of Terramid: in Akasia, she was held prisoner but escaped into the swampland home of the ferocious celanaugs; in the forest, she saved members of an itinerant band of loggers from falling to their deaths by flying up to save them; in the caverns she disappeared from sight, them reemerged as the

captain of a ship not seen for decades, the sunship. She has made small miracles happen. Witnesses speak of flight, strength, strange energies that force physical matter to bend to her will, and most important, that she can heal the sick and infirm. I prefer to believe that there is truth to these tales, no matter how outlandish.

While Sephie becomes legend down below, dark tales surround the Minister of Cadador, but I believe them also to be true. They say his touch corrupts and even kills, that destruction radiates from his passing. Ilahn has redoubled his efforts to enforce Cadador's control over all shipping and trade. Several cities have felt his anger: Akasia has been declared to be off the trade routes, although we have heard they still produce their wares; and Torbel, of course, was sacrificed to assuage Ilahn's ego. They say Ilahn is joined by a woman who commands lightning that springs from her fingers, a tiny oracle who advises him in his dealings, and a man who hails from another world. If these stories are even partly true, life on our world may be reduced to an apocalyptic clash between these two forces — the destruction at Minister Ilahn's command, and the renewing sprit of Minister Sephie.

Sephie's mark is a swirling of golden winds within a compass-pointed sun. Her ship is a design never before seen on Demetria. Her crew, volunteers all, come from many cities and have dedicated their lives to her cause: the equalization of trade relations between the sky cities and the surface ones. She has become an inspiration to all people of good spirit, even if her current path seems a mite harsh — her crew stops all trade, just to prove Ilahn's forces can be challenged, before moving on without incident, but their last foray, a battle against Cadador's armada, had casualties despite Sephie's willingness to use her gifts to heal the enemy.

Sephie fights to unite us; Ilahn moves to defeat us. With otherworldly energies abounding and strange new visitors coming to Demetria, I fear for our world should Sephie not prove strong enough to triumph over Ilahn.

And me, I betray my optimism by writing to children yet unborn that I plan to have by a father yet unchosen. I hope that we may someday read this book together, laughing at my fears as we share memories of the wonders and trials that are yet to be.

With love,

Laolara

CROSSGEN COMICS

Graphic Novels

THE FIRST 1	Two Houses Divided	$19.95	1-931484-04-X
THE FIRST 2	Magnificent Tension	$19.95	1-931484-17-1
MYSTIC 1	Rite of Passage	$19.95	1-931484-00-7
MYSTIC 2	The Demon Queen	$19.95	1-931484-06-6
MYSTIC 3	Siege of Scales	$15.95	1-931484-24-4
MERIDIAN 1	Flying Solo	$19.95	1-931484-03-1
MERIDIAN 2	Going to Ground	$19.95	1-931484-09-0
MERIDIAN 3	Taking the Skies	$15.95	1-931484-21-X
SCION 1	Conflict of Conscience	$19.95	1-931484-02-3
SCION 2	Blood for Blood	$19.95	1-931484-08-2
SCION 3	Divided Loyalties	$15.95	1-931484-26-0
SIGIL 1	Mark of Power	$19.95	1-931484-01-5
SIGIL 2	The Marked Man	$19.95	1-931484-07-4
SIGIL 3	The Lizard God	$15.95	1-931484-28-7
CRUX 1	Atlantis Rising	$15.95	1-931484-14-7
NEGATION 1	Bohica	$19.95	1-931484-30-9
SOJOURN 1	From the Ashes	$19.95	1-931484-15-5
SOJOURN 2	The Dragon's Tale	$15.95	1-931484-34-1
RUSE 1	Enter the Detective	$15.95	1-931484-19-8
THE PATH 1	Crisis of Faith	$19.95	1-931484-32-5
CROSSGEN ILLUSTRATED Volume 1		$24.95	1-931484-05-8

Meridian

Trade Paperback

Vol. 1 2 &3